MYSTERY AT POINT BEACH

~ Book 2 ~

Pirate's Booty

Kate Jungwirth

Deborah Erdmann

Printed in the United States of America

First Printing, 2018

ISBN- 9781728740867

Cover design by: Henry Kiryowa Luja and Kawooya Tonny of Bulamu Art Community

This book is dedicated to:

My dad, who taught me how to fish

and let me steer the boat—

even after hitting a few rocks ~ KJ

Wyatt and Faith,

the inspiration for Forest and Sailor

~ DE

CHAPTER 1

"Ahoy, matey! Swab the deck, scallywags!" *Arrrr …*

"Pipe down, Pedro. I'm going camping, not sailing the seven seas." Mom bought me a Macaw because she thought I might be lonely. I have to admit, having a parrot does add a lot of noise to a room.

I continued rummaging through the garage for my latest eBay purchase. Shelves of paint cans, sports equipment, and memorabilia stacked from floor to ceiling slowed down my search.

"Ah, here it is." I grabbed the metal detector, a small metal shovel, and my backpack just as I heard GB laying on the horn outside. "GB" is my nickname for Grandpa Bob. "Mom!" I hollered into the house. "Can you come get Pedro?"

She made her way into the garage, took off her apron and held out her hand. The parrot flapped his massive green wings, circling the garage a few times before happily landing onto her extended finger. "Vote for Pedro! Vote for Pedro!" *Squaaawwk!*

"Have fun camping, Dominic. Behave yourself for Grandpa." Mom handed me my Green Bay Packer cap and opened the door a crack, careful not to let Pedro fly out. "Oh, and don't worry … I remembered to pack your bunny slippers."

I squeezed my eyes shut. *Ugh, why does she always embarrass me like that?*

GB climbed out of his old, rusty truck to help me load my bike. Talk about embarrassment …

"What planet did *that* outfit come from?"

"Just something I saved up in the attic. I wanted to surprise Windsong and join the hippie reunion on the group site." GB's tie-dyed T-shirt and bandana took the expression "far out" to the extreme.

I was excited when my friends Forest and Sailor called to say they were joining us at Point Beach, but their grandma, Windsong, could be a bad influence on GB sometimes. This was a prime example.

"Don't tell me you want to be a hippie, now?" I

complained. The smell of mothballs filled the air as we drove off; his striped pants burning my retinas all the way to Point Beach.

Fifteen polka tunes later, we finally reached the campground. I gave a sigh of relief to see a young woman at the office window and not Ranger Rick. He gave us so much grief last summer that I crossed my fingers and made a wish he was gone.

"It's beautiful weather for camping." Leaning out the window with our ticket, the young lady glanced behind us. "Is that a Nimrod? Oh, wow. My parents used to own one of those campers. It's an antique!"

Worst possible thing to say to GB.

He gave her an unappreciative frown. "Come on, ole' Nelly." GB coaxed the stuttering engine as we pulled through the parking lot.

Lumbering down the road surrounded by trees and fresh air, we drove up to site #127, our favorite site in the park.

All that was left was to back in the trailer. We had this down to a science.

I grabbed my walkie-talkie and hopped out.

"Let me know if I'm headed for the rhubarb," GB said into his radio.

"Say what, now?" I replied.

" —the ditch."

GB cranked the wheel left, slowly maneuvering Nimrod backward while I directed him. Things were going good until a station wagon pulling a gaudy, lime- green camper with bright pink curtains drove up behind us and distracted me from my post.

"Watch out for that tree!" A familiar voice hollered from the passenger seat, nearly running GB off the pavement.

"You're in the rhubarb! You're in the rhubarb!" I yelled into my walkie-talkie.

GB screeched to a halt.

I turned back to see Forest, grinning like a fool and Sailor wildly waving her arms from the back seat. I was thrilled to see they made it.

"Hi, boys … isn't she a beauty?" Grandma Windsong stopped in the middle of the road, hopped down from the driver's seat, and held out her arms toward the trailer, Vanna White style. "I got it for a bargain, and the owners even threw in a canopy and a grill."

Forest jumped out of the car with Sailor on his heels.

"Well, I see Nimrod survived another year."

"Of course. What'd you expect?" I gave him a slug for making fun of our canvas pop-up camper.

"Aren't you supposed to be setting up on the group site?" GB put the truck in park and stepped down to check out Windsong's new wheels.

I held my breath while Forest tried hard not to laugh.

"Awesome getup, Bobby." Windsong clapped her hands. "I really dig the groovy outfit. Too bad the reunion was canceled this year." She flipped back her silver-streaked hair. "But the good news is, we lucked out and got the site next door."

"I wouldn't call it luck," Sailor said. "You know how persistent Windsong is. She was on the phone with Reserve America trying to get site #125, but the agent said it wasn't available. Windsong's like … 'It has to be. Click the button, click the button. For the love of God click the button!'"

"Yeah, so the guy says he knows how to click buttons—it's his job to click buttons," Forest added. "Then *he* clicked a button. He hung up on her."

I laughed. "That's hilarious."

"I kept calling until someone must've canceled, and here we are. My persistence paid off." Windsong took the ribbing in stride, laughing along with us until a few vehicles started lining up behind our entourage.

She hurried back in and took the wheel. "Do you mind if Forest and Sailor stay here while I get our camper situated?"

"Sure, unless you need help," GB offered.

"Thanks, Bobby." Windsong winked. "I think I can handle it."

As soon as GB cranked up Nimrod, he hurried inside—probably to find something else to wear.

"What's this doohicky?" Sailor spotted my metal

detector and started pushing it back and forth across the gravel road. "Look at me. I'm a maid."

"Be careful!" I nearly choked. "I spent a lot of money on that."

"Ha, ha. Seriously, Dominic? What are you going to do, vacuum the beach?" Forest smirked as Sailor continued her antics, running around with it like a stick pony.

"Hey, stop …" I tried to snatch it away from her, but she was too quick.

"I know," Sailor blurted, "I bet it's a weed whacker."

"What? Don't either of you know what a metal detector is?" I raised my hands. "I thought it would be fun to look for treasure on the beach."

GB stepped out of the camper dressed like an old man again instead of a hippie. "When I was growing up, if I needed money, I did something your generation is unfamiliar with."

"What's that?" I asked.

"It's called work." GB proceeded to fill our heads

with stories about how he had to pull weeds out of the neighbor's field for a dime a day, and walk five miles uphill both ways, delivering newspapers.

No wonder he's always so grumpy.

"Well, that was a hundred years ago, and besides, we're only twelve years old," I said.

"Speak for yourself, Dominic. I'm thirteen and a half." Forest puffed out his chest.

How could I forget? "Anyways, do you guys want to see how it works?"

Sailor handed the metal detector back to me. I turned it on, listening to the blips and bleeps as I probed back and forth over a bare spot on the ground. Lines pulsed across the screen until a solid bar formed, indicating a metal object below.

Sailor and Forest stood with eyes wide as I vigorously scooped away the dirt with my shovel.

"Got it!" I yelled, but my excitement quickly dimmed.

"Wow, a bottle cap," Forest scoffed. "I would leap in the air to click my heels, but then all the change would fall out of my pockets."

"Well, I didn't say it would be easy. Let's head down to the beach. Stuff washes up on the shore all the time." I handed Forest the shovel.

"Don't be gone too long. Dinner will be ready soon." GB proceeded to set up the grill.

"Radio me when it's done." I grabbed a walkie-talkie as we took off over a steep hill of sand and junipers toward Lake Michigan.

On the other side of the ridge, we came to an abrupt stop. Ribbons of yellow "DO NOT CROSS" tape stretched through the dunes, designating what appeared to be an excavation site.

"Guys, look what happened to the fort." I pointed to a pile of sticks and branches scattered on the shore. It was our meeting place last year when we solved the ice cream mystery, but now only a caved-in shell remains.

"Who would do such a thing?" Sailor fumed.

I sighed, setting my metal detector down on a log. "I don't know, but there's nothing we can do about it now … unless we fix it?"

"That would take all day," Forest objected.

"Aw come on. A little hard work never killed anybody—remember what GB said." I reached for a nearby branch.

"Yeah, but why should I take a chance?" Forest crossed his arms. "I'll keep hunting for buried treasure on the beach while you two play pick-up-sticks."

"Fine." I turned on my detector and handed it to him while Sailor and I tried to piece together a structure that somewhat resembled the old fort.

The hot July sun slowed our progress. I was tempted to take a break and dip my toes into the cool lake water. Then I heard it—

Blip, blip …. Beep, beep, beep, beep …

"I found something!" Forest yelled.

CHAPTER 2

I ran over by Forest. to see what the fuss was about. Sure enough, the screen on my metal detector lit up in his hands. I grabbed the shovel, furiously scooping away at the sand.

"What are you doing, digging a hole to China?" Sailor leaned over my shoulder to get a closer look.

"It seems that way." I paused to wipe the sweat from my brow.

Finally, a flat object loosened beneath the blade. I lifted up the star-shaped piece of metal and brushed it off on my shorts. "I think it's a badge of some sort. It looks really old." I handed it to Forest.

I couldn't believe he discovered something that was actually cool—especially after making fun of me for bringing a metal detector in the first place.

Forest walked over to the lake, bending down to wash away the remaining sand. "I think it says, 'US

Deputy Marshal' on it." He squinted at the worn-off print.

"Speaking of which ..." Sailor pointed toward a figure coming our way as Forest quickly slipped the badge into his pocket.

It was Ranger Rick.

Dang it! He hadn't transferred to a different park after all. He'd given me a tough time last year, partly due to "Nimrod," but mostly because we got in the way of his so-called authority. I braced myself for the worst.

"Well, lookie here ... if it isn't Holmes and Watson." His grin looked positively menacing. "Pray tell, what sort of mystery will you be solving this year?"

"Maybe if you did your job, we wouldn't have to step in." Forest was treading in deep water now. I gave him the "cut off" signal, running my hand sideways across my throat, but it was too late.

"Not so fast." Ranger Rick did a double take at the sight of my metal detector. "You got a permit for that?" he asked, tipping back his oversized hat.

"No," I confessed. "Am I supposed to?"

"You bet you are. Using a metal detector on state grounds is breaking the law, so I'd better not catch you snooping around with that on government property."

"Aw, come on," Sailor protested. "Seems pretty harmless if you ask me."

"Well, no one asked you. Besides, there's enough scavenging going on at Point Beach the way it is." He put his hands on his hips. "On second thought—hand it over. You can pick it up at the office when you leave. How's that for doing my job?"

I reluctantly surrendered the metal detector and watched Ranger Rick triumphantly trudge back down the beach with my most valued possession.

"That bites." Forest took the badge out of his pocket, shining it up with his T-shirt. "At least he didn't get this. It could be worth a fortune."

"Scavengers, huh?" My wheels started to turn. "It sounds like we're not the only ones digging up stuff around here. Come on. Let's go check things out."

Forest and Sailor followed behind me single file

as we walked the narrow trail along the tree-encumbered ridge. I surveyed the shoreline until we reached the picnic grounds, with no activity in sight.

"Last one to the beach is a rotten egg!" Forest shouted. The three of us clambered down to the water's edge, skidding and sliding the whole way, startling a blue-and-silver-haired lady right out of her seat.

We stopped running when we noticed it was Sadie, the elderly camp host who volunteers here every summer. "Hi, Mrs. Buckley!"

She lowered her heart-shaped, glittery sunglasses. "Oh, my stars … I thought I was about to get trampled by a herd of wild animals, but I see it's only my three favorite detectives."

"Sorry 'bout that." Sailor couldn't keep her eyes off the stylish, Hawaiian cover-up Sadie wore over her swimsuit.

"What's Mr. Buckley up to today?" I asked. The two of them were usually inseparable.

Sadie looked around. "Hmm? He was here just a minute ago, tied to the leg of my chair."

"You have to keep him tied up?" Forest grinned.

"No, he's on a raft. Oh, dear." Sadie removed her glasses, squinting toward the lake at an inflatable duck, its yellow head flopping limply to one side, with Bert's hairy arms and legs hanging over the edge.

"There he is … Bert!" she yelled, but the inner tube kept drifting further away from shore.

"Is everything alright?" A young man in Bermuda shorts with wavy brown hair walked over to us.

"Not really." Sadie's voice went up an octave. "My husband floated off into the lake."

"Well, it doesn't look like he's coming back on his own. In fact, he could get into some trouble with the current. I'd better go after him."

"Would you please, and hurry!"

"My hero." Sailor swayed as she watched him run and dive into the waves.

Another day in the life of a diva. I shook my head.

This guy seemed pretty accustomed to the water, and it wasn't long before he returned with Mr. Buckley and the deflated duck in tow.

"What's all the commotion?" Bert complained, as he hobbled out of the water. "Can't an old guy take a snooze without being bothered?"

"You'd be in the middle of the lake by now if he hadn't rescued you." Sadie handed Bert a beach towel. A thick layer of sunscreen covered his nose and shoulders, but his bald head was bright red.

"Glad I could help. I'm Maverick, the new summer activity director at Point Beach."

She smiled at him. "We're the camp hosts at Point Beach. You're welcome to stop by site #74, anytime. And this is Mitch and his sidekicks." Sadie pointed in our direction. "They solved a mystery here last year."

"Yes … I mean, no. I'm Dominic, remember?"

Maybe I need to start wearing a nametag.

Maverick turned toward us. "Say, if you're looking for another adventure, I'm giving snorkeling lessons this weekend."

"I wouldn't miss it for the world." Sailor smiled like a goofball.

"Great. Just have a parent or guardian fill out the consent form at the office. Then you'll be all set."

"Wow … that sounds awesome. Sailor and I went snorkeling in Florida last year with our uncle." Forest raised himself on tiptoes.

"Well, this isn't Florida. We don't have coral reefs or tropical fish, but there are a few shipwrecks for experienced divers to explore. How about you, Dominic? Want to give it a try?"

"Maybe." I looked down at my feet. *Snorkeling? That didn't sound like a sane thing to do.*

"Okay, then—hope to see you soon." Maverick gave us a wink before heading to the parking lot.

Sailor gazed dreamily after him.

"Seems like a nice fella," Sadie said to Bert as she gathered her beach bag.

"So, what's up with all the holes around here?" I pointed out the mounds of sand and dirt in the picnic area.

"Ancient artifacts," Bert said bluntly while folding up their chair.

"Oh … like dinosaur bones?" Sailor asked.

"Not *that* old," Sadie corrected her. "A compass was uncovered during a sand sculpture contest a few weeks ago. It attracted treasure hunters from all over, including an archeologist, Dr. Lloyd Sogge, who insists the compass came from a shipwreck off Point Beach."

"Wow! That's awesome." My jaw dropped.

"Oh, he's a know-it-all scientist alright, always talking about his research mumbo jumbo." Bert waved his hand in dismissal.

"He even wants to pick my brain about local history for some book he's writing." She smiled, the corners of her eyes wrinkling. "You see, my father was once the lightkeeper here. I have so many wonderful memories of this place."

"And some bad ones, too." Bert coughed. "Does 'Roaring Dan' ring a bell?"

"Now, Albert," Sadie said. "That's not a tale for children. We should get going. I think you've had enough sun for one day."

"What? Come on. You can't leave us hanging like

that." Forest jammed his hands into his pockets.

"Yeah," Sailor whined. "We want to know who Roaring Dan is. He sounds like a big bully."

Sadie began gathering her suntan lotions, snacks and towels and stuffed them into her beach bag. "More than that—he was a pirate."

CHAPTER 3

"Roaring Dan was infamous in these parts. He stole an entire ship—chained up the captain and threw him overboard." Bert spit into the sand. "There's even a legend he buried treasure nearby."

"Now, now, those are only rumors. Don't bother the children with such nonsense," Sadie scolded.

"Are you kidding me?" I began to wonder if a pirate had actually roamed Point Beach.

"Perhaps you can talk to Dr. Sogge about it tonight. He's coming over for a campfire. I'm sure he has plenty of stories to tell," Sadie offered.

"We'd love to!" I spoke for all of us.

"Wonderful." She put on a wide-brimmed hat. "Now we really have to go. Bert needs some *Aloe vera*."

"What's that about *marinara?*" Bert asked.

"I said, 'You-need-some-*Aloe-vera*.'"

He frowned. "What about the spaghetti?"

Sadie clobbered him over the head with her hat.

"Be careful—I'm sunburned!" Bert winced as he followed Sadie to their golf cart.

"Did you hear that? A pirate at Point Beach? We're gonna be rich!" Sailor danced in circles.

"Too bad Ranger Rick confiscated your metal detector," Forest said.

"Yeah. Too bad." I picked up a seashell and threw it at him. My walkie-talkie started to beep.

"This is Dominator, over."

Kwwwittchhh …

"GB here. Change of plans. Windsong made dinner. Meet me at site #125. Over."

"I thought you were cooking on the grill. What are we having?"

"Your choice … 'take it' or 'leave it.' Over and out." The radio clicked and GB went silent.

"We'd better get going. All this talk of pirate's treasure is making me hungry."

I led the way down the road, following the aroma of campfire smoke floating off the lake breeze until we reached site #125. Neon flower lights were strung around the overhead canopy with one of Windsong's woven rugs covering the grass beneath the picnic table.

"Come on, kids. There's plenty of food here." Windsong motioned to a variety of organic goodies spread out on a pink-checkered cloth.

"Thanks, but we need to make this quick. The Buckleys invited us to meet their special guest, Dr. Lloyd Sogge. He's researching a pirate compass that was found on the beach." I passed on the salad and started with crackers spread with ho-hummus something or other.

"Doctor who?" GB scratched his head.

"Just some professor who looks at old junk and tells fairytales," Forest said.

One bite from my cracker and I already needed a drink to help me choke it down. "Do you have any Orange Crush?"

Forest pushed his blonde bangs out of his eyes. "You're still stuck on orange? You know they make hundreds of other flavors, right?"

"I'll stop drinking Orange Crush when you stop wearing jeans in the middle of summer."

Windsong shrugged. "Sorry, all I have is water or fresh-squeezed lemonade."

How do they survive?

"Lemonade, please," I grumbled.

"Dominic's bummed out because the ranger took his metal detector. He said you need a permit for it." Forest poured himself some lemonade, not bothering to mention the badge he'd found.

"What kind of catawampus ..." GB's color drained from his face. "I'll need to have a word with that ranger."

"Oh, and guess what else?" Sailor blurted out. "The new instructor, Maverick, saved Mr. Buckley from floating off into the lake today."

"It wasn't that big a deal. Sailor's just in loooove." Forest made goo-goo eyes at her.

"I am not!" She stuck out her tongue at him. "Maverick said we should sign up for snorkeling to-morrow. Can we, pleeease?"

"Well, it sounds like you kids have plenty of activities planned." GB gathered our empty plates and cups. "But first you can help with the dishes."

I carried a stack of plates inside the slime-mobile, placing them on a lime green countertop that matched the cabinet doors of the kitchenette. Pastel-flowered cushions and pillows covered the bench seats.

"Maybe we can use our camper as home base this year?" Sailor suggested.

"What, and retire Nimrod? Your camper may be hip, but Nimrod's been known to inspire great minds." I tapped my forehead.

Forest groaned. "I hope your *great mind* isn't planning on spending our entire vacation trying to solve mysteries again."

"Either that, or we can organize Sailor's stuffed animal collection." I marveled at the mountainous pile of fuzzy creatures on one of the beds.

Sailor immersed her hands in the sudsy water at the sink. "Those aren't all mine. Some are Forest's."

"They are not!" He snapped a towel at her.

"Can you two quit fooling around and help? I want to get to the Buckleys before it's past their bedtime."

"At their age, that's probably eight o'clock." Forest laughed as he finished drying the last dish.

I glanced at the time. It was quarter to eight. I opened the screen door. "GB, it's time to go!" *Ugh, what's the holdup?*

"Hold your horses, Dominic. Windsong asked if I'd check the oil in her car." He lifted the hood as the three of us piled out the door.

"Can you hurry? I want to bring along my s'mores ingredients." I doubted the Buckleys had the proper supplies.

"I'm sure they'll appreciate your strawberry and chocolate marshmallows." GB rubbed his hands with a rag. "This will only take a few minutes."

"Oh, goody. That means I still have time to paint my nails." Sailor held her hands out. "I think I'll do pink with red flowers this time." She ran back inside.

Has the whole world gone mad?

When we approached the camp host site, Mrs. Buckley saw us coming and scampered from chair to chair, wiping away pinecones and forest debris. Some of the leaves found their way into the blue nest of hair on her head.

Sailor took off after Sprinkles, the Buckleys' beloved miniature poodle, trying to get the poor pooch to stay still long enough to cuddle with it.

"I'm so glad you could join us tonight." Sadie smoothed out the palm leaf patterns in her dress.

"Let me help you with that." Windsong started wiping the remaining chairs. "I just love what you've done with the place. The Tropicana décor makes me feel like I'm in Florida."

This is so not Florida.

"Well, thank you, Windmill." Sadie gushed at the compliment. "Have you noticed our new pink flamingos?" She pointed out the plastic birds planted alongside the host sign. Windsong nodded in approval, ignoring Mrs. Buckley's mix-up on her name.

The electric palm trees lit up just as the sun began setting.

"Please take a seat, everyone." Sadie walked over to the camper door, peeking inside. "Bert! Dr. Lloyd! We have guests."

I set my selection of marshmallows, cinnamon graham crackers, and white and dark chocolate bars on a tray. Dr. Lloyd was about to experience s'mores—Wisconsin style.

Bert emerged from the camper clad in his usual overalls, followed by a strange-looking character with bushy hair, a mustache, and dark-rimmed glasses.

"Everyone, this is Dr. Lloyd Sogge," Sadie announced. "He's doing research at Point Beach."

Dr. Lloyd wore a short-sleeved, button-down shirt with a plaid bowtie—not the typical camp attire I was used to. He sure stood out in a crowd.

Sailor stopped chasing Sprinkles and approached

him. "Hello, Mr. Soggy."

"You can call me Dr. Lloyd. People get confused about my last name. It's pronounced SAH-gee." He cleared his throat, lifting his bold glasses up from his nose to get a better look at her. "You folks came to see the latest tourist attraction, I presume?"

"Actually, we're camping. I'm Dominic." I walked over and held out my hand toward Dr. Lloyd, anxious to meet him. He shook it, then immediately reached in his front pocket for hand sanitizer.

"The children were interested in hearing about some of your latest escapades." Sadie clasped her hands together. "We told them you were writing a book on Pirate Dan Seavey."

Dr. Lloyd's bulging grey eyes turned, locking onto us. "What would you like to know? A man of my expertise has plenty to talk about."

Expertise? Apparently, the exotic marshmallow and cracker flavors went right over his head.

"Mrs. Buckley promised you'd tell us pirate stories." Sailor sat upright in her seat.

"Not stories, young lady — they're very real." Dr. Lloyd stared at her. He acted a bit odd, but I supposed he didn't get out much with all his studies.

"Who's ready for marshmallows?" GB began whittling the tip of a stick with his pocketknife.

The sky began to darken, revealing a full moon, while a small group of black crows took up residence in a nearby pine tree, beady eyes glaring. Suddenly, the biggest bird in the tree swooped in our direction, taking a swing at the nest on Sadie's head.

CHAPTER 4

"Lord have mercy!" Sadie cried, nearly collapsing into the fire pit while shielding her head from the crow.

Bert grabbed hold of her in the nick of time, which was surprising. I've never seen the old guy come to life like that before.

"Keep away, you wacky bird!" Bert shouted, shaking his fist at the crow. The black bird flew off, disappearing into the night sky.

"Are you okay, dear?" Windsong quickly ran to Sadie.

"I'm fine, just a little shook up." She dusted herself off. After calming down from the bird attack, she retrieved a kettle of hot water, pouring it into cups for mixing hot chocolate.

I went out on a limb and put a strawberry marshmallow in mine.

Unfazed by the commotion, Dr. Lloyd moved

closer to the fire, his eyeglasses reflecting the leaping flames.

"Now, if I may ... let's begin with a pirate who sailed Lake Michigan, named Daniel Seavey, otherwise known as 'Roaring Dan.'" He glanced around the circle in a secretive manner.

"I thought pirates sailed the oceans, not lakes." Forest crossed his arms.

"Well, you're wrong, my boy." Dr. Lloyd removed his glasses, polishing them on his polyester shirt. "At one time, the Great Lakes were almost as dangerous as the Wild West, partly thanks to Seavey's reputation."

"What was a pirate doing around here?" I asked, still unclear how he and the compass related to Point Beach.

"That's what I aim to find out. It's like putting together a very old puzzle. Some pieces are missing, others don't seem to fit, but I'm hoping Mrs. Buckley can help, seeing as her father knew Dan personally."

"I guess you could say that." Sadie reached for

her cup. "My father was Charlie Vinnette, one of the last lightkeepers at Point Beach. He told me a few stories about the old mariner, but I never believed him much."

"What kind of stories?" I moved to the edge of my seat.

"Hmm, I believe I remember one," she paused. "When my dad was a boy, he liked to fish off the dock in Two Rivers. One day, he wasn't catching anything, so when Dan's ship came into port, he tried to steal an apple from the cargo."

"Young rascal. I'd take my hairbrush and teach him a lesson." Bert slapped his hand across his knee.

"Albert! That's my dad you're talking about," Sadie scolded. He sheepishly looked to the ground.

"Yeah, and what would *you* need a hairbrush for, anyway?" Sailor stared at his bald head.

Windsong covered Sailor's mouth with her hand. "Go on, Sadie. We're listening."

"Now, where was I?" She thought for a moment. "Oh yes, as I recall, one of the crew chased after him with a paddle. Luckily, Dan Seavey intervened. He took my dad aside, offering him root beer and ice cream if he promised he would never steal again."

"Seems like Roaring Dan had a change of heart." Sailor hugged herself.

"I never heard of a pirate with a soft spot." Forest rolled his eyes.

"Perhaps Seavey settled down as he got older," Dr. Lloyd remarked, "but a dreadful reputation followed him, that's for sure."

"I suppose there's a little good and bad in all of us." GB finally handed out the roasting sticks. I loaded mine with vanilla, chocolate, and strawberry marshmallows and lowered it over the fire.

"Please, Dr. Lloyd. Tell us more," Sailor begged. "What did the pirate look like? Did he have a patch over one eye, or a stick-leg and a parrot?" she rambled. "Oh, and what about his ship—did it wave a pirate flag?"

"Such imagination." He shook his head. "Dan was a large, strapping man, over six feet tall with a barrel chest and powerful hands. He could be quite intimidating like a pirate—I'll give you that. You couldn't help but notice him. His ship looked like any other on the lake, except for the cannon on board. It was a schooner named *Wanderer*."

"Wait a minute … if Dan already had a ship, then why did he decide to steal another one and throw the captain overboard?" I asked.

"Slow down, Strawberry Marshmallow." Forest turned his attention back to Dr. Lloyd. "That's what Mr. Buckley told us, but did it really happen?"

"It's still open to interpretation as to how Dan obtained the *Nellie Johnson* from Captain R. J. McCormick. However, there *is* one thing the reports all agree on—he stole it for one reason and one reason only—"

I leaned forward. We were all captivated, except for Bert, who steadily slouched and had started dozing off.

"—pirate's booty." Dr. Lloyd sat back.

"Cool! Did they ever catch Roaring Dan?" Sailor licked the gooey marshmallow off her sticky fingers.

"Indeed, they did." Dr. Lloyd nodded. "After a three-day cat-and-mouse chase around the lake, the Coast Guard cutter, *Tuscarora*, managed to overtake the pirate only a short distance off Point Beach."

"Oh, yes," Sadie recalled. "It was the keeper here at Twin River Point Light, as it was called back then, who alerted them."

"So, what happened to the ship?" I asked.

"It's an unsolved mystery." Dr. Lloyd pushed his glasses up his nose. "The rumor is she caught fire and sank. My greatest endeavor is to find her, and the compass gives me hope that she's nearby."

I suddenly realized my marshmallows were a little too close to the flames. I quickly lifted the roasting stick, but all that was left was a charred blob.

"Too bad it was so long ago," Sadie sighed. "There's no way of knowing for certain what really happened anymore."

"Still, the news was sensational at the time. It even went nationwide." Dr. Lloyd wrinkled his forehead, which made it look like he had one big bushy eyebrow. "Hopefully, the compass will unlock a clue."

"I have to say, this is all very impressive." Windsong pressed her palms to her cheeks. "You certainly are quite knowledgeable, Dr. Lloyd."

"I should be. I have degrees in anthropology, history, and archeology," he gloated. "I've been doing research on Roaring Dan for years. He was a real swashbuckler."

"What's that?" Sailor crinkled her nose.

"An adventurer, young lady. Not only was Seavey a pirate, but he led expeditions to ancient Indian grounds, sailed through Death's Door in hurricane-force winds, traveled to the Klondike, and was even a deputy for a while."

This is the kind of stuff you see on TV!

In my excitement, I grabbed Forest's arm. The jolt spilled his hot chocolate onto his lap. Judging by the scathing look he gave me, if Forest were wearing an eye patch, I'd be swabbing the poop deck right now.

"How thrilling!" Windsong twirled her peace-sign necklace. "The biggest adventure I had in my lifetime was a weekend at Woodstock. That was a wild scene."

At that, Bert let out a gigantic snore that startled us half to death. It seemed to scare him as well.

"Well, I think it's time to go." GB put his hand on my shoulder. "We shouldn't overstay our welcome."

"Aw, do we have to?" I whined.

"Don't make me get out my hairbrush." GB chuckled, running his hand over his thinning grey hair. "Besides, we need to wake up early for our own expedition. We're going charter fishing."

"Really?" I cheered up a little.

"Can we go, too?" Forest and Sailor pleaded with Windsong.

She shook her head. "One foot on a boat and I turn green as guacamole. I thought a nice trip to the Rogers Street Fishing Museum would be fun."

"We can all meet for ice cream sundaes, afterward," GB proposed.

"I guess so." Sailor frowned, wrapping her arms around her waist.

"The children are welcome to stop by the Rawley Point vacation house whenever they please," Dr. Lloyd suggested as we got up to leave. "It would benefit them greatly to be under my wing. In fact, Dominic reminds me of myself when I was just a lad—full of curiosity and vision." He straightened both ends of his bow tie.

Was that supposed to be a compliment? I shuddered at the comparison.

"Wait a minute … what about the pirate's booty?" Forest asked. "You never told us what happened to it."

"I can't give away all my secrets, now can I?" Dr. Lloyd produced a strange, crooked grin that made me even more curious.

CHAPTER 5

Ribbons of bright red and orange blazed across the horizon of the sleepy town of Two Rivers as we entered the Seagull Marina. The only early risers were local fishermen gathering their equipment on the wooden docks that jutted out into the West Twin River.

GB and I stepped into the small office; its walls adorned with a few mounted trophy fish.

A girl with black-dyed hair and a pierced nose welcomed us. "I hope you have a great time," she said after checking our confirmation number.

"How's the fishing, lately?" GB asked.

She looked around, lowering her voice. "Between you and me … it's been better."

Just then, the phone rang.

"Good luck!" She rested the phone on her shoulder as we headed for the door. "You're gonna need it."

The sun reflected off the waves like diamonds. I slipped on my life jacket and pulled out my sunglasses before walking up to the boat.

"Welcome to *Willie Bee* Charter Service. I'm Captain Bill." A muscular man with a grizzly red beard gave me a firm handshake as I climbed onboard.

"I'm not gonna fall in, right?" I tipped to the side as the ship rocked against the dock but caught myself.

"Don't worry," he reassured me. "I haven't lost anyone, yet."

GB and I sat down on swivel seats while the captain started the engine, turning on his GPS to pinpoint our destination.

"Can we try fishing over by Point Beach?" My detective mind wanted to do double-duty.

"That's typically been a good spot, so long as we don't get snagged on a shipwreck," the captain said as he swung the boat around. "They don't call Rawley Point 'the graveyard of the lake' for nothing."

"I understand there's quite a few down there." GB looked grim.

Captain Bill tipped his cap. "In those days, before the lighthouse was constructed, navigation was difficult, especially during a squall. Many ships foundered on the shoals, battered to pieces by the waves."

"What happened to the men onboard?" My stomach felt queasy against the chop of the waves.

"Sink, swim, or be rescued," Captain Bill explained. "That's why they began a lifesaving station in Two Rivers, which is now the Coast Guard."

Sailing an old, creaky ship sure seems like risky business. Good thing I had my life jacket on.

Captain Bill stopped the boat, and we dropped our lines. I learned all about downriggers, outriggers, spoons, and fly rigs as we trolled back and forth, but nothing would take the bait.

"It's been a rough year," Captain Bill admitted after about an hour. "We have some of the best sporting holes in the Midwest, but water levels are at a record low, and the fish are hard to find."

He studied his GPS and depth finder as we motored over the open water around Point Beach.

"Do you think you could locate a sunken ship with that?" I asked, louder than intended.

"You need sonar or a magnetometer—a type of underwater metal detector for that kind of job. Most wrecks are hundreds of feet below the surface where only trained divers can go."

"Next thing you know, Dominic will want to give it a try." GB nodded in my direction. "He might even learn how to snorkel later today."

"There are a few shipwrecks close to shore, but you have to be careful," Captain Bill warned. "These waters can be very dangerous. I've seen records of waves that were higher than a two-story building."

"Whoa." I grabbed hold of my seat, my knuckles turning white.

"That sounds almost as incredible as the rumor going around Point Beach about some pirate and a compass," GB said. "It even brought in an archeologist who's staying at the lighthouse."

"Yer looking for me treasure, aye, matey?" Captain Bill curled his upper lip, letting out a low, baritone laugh. His pirate imitation reminded me of Pedro.

"So there really is trea—" I started to say, when my fishing pole jerked hard, pulling me to the floor as I hung on for dear life.

"You got one!" Captain Bill yelled. "Keep a bend on it now, and don't give any slack."

The reel began to reverse, violently unwinding. I was dragged to the ship's railing, which was the only thing that saved me from going overboard.

"Dominic, hold your ground!" GB came alongside me.

The fish was getting closer. I continued to pull in the lunker, until a spiked fin breached the top of the water, thrashing around in a frenzy all the way up to the boat.

"Here it comes …" Captain Bill dipped a landing net below the stern, pulling up a silver-scaled fish. "It's a king salmon. Probably close to 30 pounds!"

"What a dandy! Let me get a picture." GB focused his camera while I tried to hold the slippery salmon that spanned from the floor to my hip.

Captain Bill took it from me, removing a green flasher-flyer out of the fish's sharp teeth with pliers.

"My arms feel like rubber." I gave them a rest while the captain wound up the excess line and set the rod back in the stand.

"Looks like you got a bonus," he said. Reaching over the side, he grabbed a white buoy with some tangled line wrapped around it. "The salmon snagged a shipwreck marker."

I searched the water, surprised to be able to see so well through the waves. As we continued to drift closer to shore, a large, dark shadow appeared beneath us, bigger than a whale.

Could it be a sunken ship?

CHAPTER 6

I leaned over to get a better look at the structure on the lake floor, until I heard the sound of an engine getting closer. I looked up just in time to see a red and white boat cut in front of us, sending a large wake against the *Willie Bee*'s hull. A wall of icy water came crashing over the side, soaking me from head to toe.

"Hold on, Dominic!" GB grabbed my life vest by the strap, pulling me back inside, away from the edge.

"Crazy driver!" Captain Bill scowled as the boat sped past.

"I'm okay." I clung to the railing, frozen in place.

They both had a good laugh at my expense.

"I'll never do *that* again." My teeth chattered while I crouched in my seat, wrapped in a towel. Still, I wondered if the splintered beams I saw sticking out of the sand were part of a shipwreck.

"I suppose we should head back. Besides, that

fish should be plenty for the two of us." GB took one more picture of me before the *Willie Bee* prepared to leave.

When we reached the marina, Captain Bill climbed out and moored the boat to the dock. "I hope you enjoyed the trip," he said, after securing the line.

"Thanks, Captain. It was epic!" I stepped onto the boardwalk, but my body swayed like I was still on the water.

"Well, Dominic, are you ready to meet the rest of our crew for some ice cream?" GB stuffed his sunglasses into his shirt pocket.

"I sure am." I licked my parched lips. I couldn't wait to tell my friends about what I saw, though Forest would probably think it was a whale of a tale.

The captain brought over a carefully wrapped package of fish filets. GB placed them in a cooler, pouring a small bag of ice over the top. "This is going to taste great with lemon pepper seasoning."

My mouth watered, just thinking about the fish sizzling over a campfire. This almost made the fact that

I got soaking wet and chilled to the bone worth it.

"Oh, and don't forget your souvenir." Captain Bill leaned over and handed me the buoy. The words 'Diving Adventures' ran across the top.

As I rolled it around in my hands, I noticed a sequence of letters and numbers in permanent ink.

N 44° 12.454' W 87° 30.211'

GB shook his head as he looked around. "Geez, Louise. It's getting to be a zoo around here." Trailers and boats came and went, making the busy marina quite congested.

My eyes caught a petite woman with silky black hair and dark-bronzed skin in a wetsuit. She was hauling scuba gear out of a red and white Crestliner, with *Thirsty Tiger* written across the back. It looked like the same boat that caused me to nearly go for a swim.

Captain Bill frowned. "I doubt they're going fishing—probably heard about the treasure, just like your archeologist friend—nothing but made-up stories to lure crazy tourists, if you ask me."

Well, then, consider me a crazy tourist.

Forest, Sailor, and I huddled over our Cedar Crest ice cream at a corner table at the Washington House Museum—last year's crime scene.

Forest studied the coordinates on the marker while wolfing down a strawberry sundae. "And you think this leads to the sunken ship?"

I nodded, licking caramel off my spoon. Picking the flavor "Pirate's Bounty" was a no-brainer. "Whatever's down there, I want to keep it secret. Divers are swarming the marina, and this buoy might lead to the wreck Dr. Lloyd's looking for, or even the treasure."

"I don't know ..." Forest passed it back to me. "That sounds pretty far-fetched."

"Not really." Sailor took dainty bites from a sprinkle-covered cone. "The director at the fishing museum said they find all kinds of stuff on shipwrecks."

"Like what?" I asked.

"Ummm, I forgot." She rubbed her temple.

"Looks like Sailor got brain freeze." Forest elbowed me.

"Oh, honey, are you alright?" Windsong sat down next to her with a small dish of yogurt.

"I'm fine. I was just telling Dominic about the sunken ships. He's really interested in all that."

"Maybe you'd like to borrow the book I picked up at the museum?" Windsong reached into her satchel and handed me *Treasures of the Great Lakes*. "It reveals a few mysteries connected with some of the shipwrecks buried beneath the waves."

"We could even read it around the campfire." Sailor licked her lips. "It sounds spooky, like going through a haunted house, underwater."

"Are you two going bonkers? We're on summer vacation—the word 'reading' shouldn't even be in our vocabulary right now," Forest groaned.

"When I was your age, we read books for fun," Windsong said.

I studied the shipwreck on the cover—buried in

sand and surrounded by murky lake water. "Thanks, Windsong. I'll return it before we leave."

"No problem, Dominic. How was the boat ride?" She swirled a spoon around in her yogurt, mixing in the strawberry sauce.

"I nearly threw up my Fruit Loops."

"That would've been quite the show!" Forest chuckled.

"At least I caught a fish, and Captain Bill gave me a souvenir."

GB came back with his usual dish of plain vanilla, only this time there was a cherry on top. "Sorry, Dominic, but Diving Adventures is right around the corner from here. We'll be returning your 'souvenir' just as soon as we're done."

"Geez, GB. Do you really think they care?" *He always wants to do the right thing — it's so annoying.*

After finishing my ice cream, I made sure to excuse myself so I could copy the coordinates onto a napkin, just in case.

GB and I pulled up to the curb in front of Diving Adventures, with Windsong parking behind us. A large, red kayak projecting from the roof singled it out from the other stores nearby.

We stepped inside, weaving through racks of wetsuits, fins, life vests and other equipment before reaching the front desk. A middle-aged man with a bleach-blonde crew cut and dimples sat behind a stack of opened catalogs, talking on the phone as we waited.

"Yes … to explore the *Continental*. I have a group going out at three o'clock. I just need your name and phone number," he said, writing down the infor-mation. "Thank you, Mr. Jones. See you soon. Good-bye." He hung up quickly. "How can I help you folks?"

"Well, my grandson and I are here on vacation and a funny thing happened—we went out fishing on the *Willie Bee* this morning, and did we ever have a great time. Dominic reeled in a whopper and ..."

I could tell GB was about to make a short story into a long one, so I plopped the marker on the desk alongside a display of fancy underwater watches.

"Isn't that something." The man rubbed his chin. "How'd you end up with this?"

"Dominic reeled it up on accident. Sorry about the smell," GB apologized. "It was next to a dead salmon for a while. What can you do."

The man's eyes brightened as he rotated the marker in his hands before placing it in a desk drawer. "Here's my number in case you find anything else." He handed me his business card.

Directly above the contact information in bold letters was the name DIVER DAN. I began to feel some bad vibes coming off this guy.

"And where, exactly, did you say you were fishing?" Dan leaned toward GB.

"We *didn't* say." I tried to stop the conversation.

"We were somewhere near the lighthouse off

Point Beach." GB volunteered.

"Interesting." Dan sat back down in his chair and began to busy himself looking over some maps.

"Just a minute, Bobby. What about this snorkel gear?" Windsong held up a yellow mask. "I found a bargain on clearance."

"Seriously? You mean we can get our own?" Sailor went into cheerleader mode, holding her arms above her head and circling around, kicking sideways.

"Awesome—then we can snorkel all weekend!" Forest fist bumped Sailor.

"With adult supervision, you can. I think it'll be groovy." Windsong brought a few more sets down from the shelf. "How about it, Dominic?"

"I never snorkeled before, and I don't think I want to start now."

"Quit being a fuddy-duddy," Forest teased.

"I'll get an extra in case you change your mind." Windsong handed Diver Dan three sets. "Do you have youth-sized life jackets? We need those, too."

He took down three life jackets from the wall behind him. Windsong paid in cash. He counted it twice before placing it in the register. *Cha-ching.* "Thank you, again. I hope you enjoy your stay."

As we turned to leave, a woman walked in, blocking the exit. "Excuse me!" She narrowed her eyes at me while she tried to juggle two oxygen tanks through the doorway. It was the same woman I'd seen earlier at the marina with the long black hair and bronze tan line on the *Thirsty Tiger.*

I watched from behind the store window as wet-suit woman proceeded to the front desk. To my surprise, Diver Dan brought the marker out from the drawer, making her frown turn upside down.

How convenient.

CHAPTER 7

Back at our site, GB fired up the grill, heat waves rising into the open air. "What in the world is sushi? It doesn't sound good for you." His eyes fixed on Windsong, her Bohemian skirt swishing as she hurried to gather ingredients.

"Oh, it's fine. You're going to love it." She tied a colorful scarf around her head.

"Alright," GB replied, "but I'm still going to make half the salmon into steaks."

I knew GB would have my back.

The three of us filed into Nimrod.

"Hey, guys," I lowered my voice. "Did you notice anything suspicious about the man at the diving store?"

"Nope." Sailor grabbed the Jenga game from the cabinet and started setting up a tower of lopsided, crisscrossed blocks. "Why? Did you?"

"He seemed overly interested in the buoy, and coincidently, his name is Dan."

Forest scoffed. "Not everyone named 'Dan' is a pirate."

"I know, but he's in the right business. If anyone can find a shipwreck on Lake Michigan, he'd be the one." I went first, removing an easy block from the side of the tower.

"Maybe we should tell Dr. Lloyd?" Sailor suggested, poking a block out from the middle. "He could hire Diver Dan to help find the treasure ship."

"Maybe not," I said as we each took a turn. "When GB and I were fishing, a lady on a boat called the *Thirsty Tiger* nearly ran into us. Then she showed up at Diving Adventures just as we were leaving, and I saw Diver Dan show her the shipwreck marker."

"Do you think they'll find the treasure?" Sailor poked out a piece from the bottom.

Forest started to remove a tight block from the corner. "Not unless we find it first."

"And how are we going to do that?" I stared at

the swaying tower left for me to skillfully dismantle.

"With our snorkel gear," Forest shot back. "How else?"

I shuddered at the thought. "No way, guys. The water gets really deep." I made my move, spilling the entire stack of Jenga blocks all over the table.

A gentle breeze floated over Lake Michigan. The water was light blue, turning to teal a few miles out. *A perfect day, unless you're about to do something you may live to regret.*

"Are you ready for an adventure of a lifetime?" Forest slapped me on the back.

"Can't I just watch from shore?"

"Don't worry." Windsong laid a beach blanket in the sand and opened a book. "It's easy. You'll see."

"Good afternoon, Snorkies!" Maverick sauntered

up the beach. "Who wants to have some fun?"

"I do!" Sailor ran alongside him as we made our way to the starting point of our "adventure," which might be the ending point as far as I was concerned. "We even brought our own life jackets and gear."

"Awesome. Then we're ready to go. Some of this will be a refresher, since the two of you have snorkeled before." Maverick collected our consent forms while Forest and Sailor started getting into their fins.

"Hey, Maverick, any chance you can take us out to one of those sunken ships?" Forest asked. "We heard there's a few close to shore."

"What we do today really depends on Dominic." Maverick scanned over the forms. "That's usually for more advanced snorkelers and it looks like he's had very little to no experience."

I looked down at my feet. *Talk about pressure.*

"Who knows? Some are in very shallow water. You kids might even discover one all on your own."

"Would we get to keep whatever we find on it?" I asked while Maverick put on his wet suit.

"I'm afraid not. Shipwrecks are protected by law. Anything removed from them can only be used for scientific purposes or public display."

"Like at the Rogers Street Museum," Sailor recalled.

"That's correct." Maverick smiled. "There's even a petition for this area to become part of the National Marine Sanctuary, due to the many historic wrecks on this shore."

After a few lessons on how to use the snorkeling gear, we were ready to jump in. With my life jacket tied tight, I pulled the fins over my feet and headed to the edge of the lake, where I flopped and fell on my face.

"Turn around and walk backward until you're in the water, then put the flat edges of the snorkel in your mouth and bite down," Maverick instructed. "You can do it."

Reluctantly, I took a few steps into the lake and bit down on the mouthpiece. It reminded me of the cardboard the dentist put in my mouth to take an x-ray of my teeth. I nearly gagged.

Once I was waist deep, I dipped my head below the waves and focused on breathing. A whole new world spread out before me. Sprigs of seaweed grew out of the sandy bottom amid a few rocks and shells. The water was not a bright blue anymore, but more of a murky grey with tiny particles floating in it.

A small silver fish, about the length of my finger, swam by. It studied me with large eyes set behind a nearly vertical mouth. Tiny fins swirled in the water until it wiggled its tail to get away and disappeared.

Taking the fish's lead, I finally found the courage to pull my feet out from under me. Normally, I'm a pretty good swimmer, but this wasn't a pool and multi-tasking isn't my specialty.

I tried to breathe through the tube, but suddenly it filled with water, forcing me to kick my way back up. I sputtered and wheezed. "Guys, I don't think I can do this."

"What are you talking about?" Forest splashed at me. "Of course you can."

Maverick lifted his mask, pushing back his long, wet bangs. "You got this, Dominic. It just takes a little practice."

"Okay. I'll try it again." I really didn't want to, but I had to find the shipwreck. That was the only reason I'd put myself in the middle of this foolishness.

Maverick motioned for Sailor and Forest to stay close as they put their snorkels back in. Side by side, they rhythmically paddled their feet, cutting through the foaming waves as they rolled in. Their flippers went above the water like dolphins as they dove.

I decided to go for it. I gripped the rubber edges of the mouthpiece as I forced myself under the water and started kicking. Surprisingly, I found myself moving along, and quite happily, I might add.

I can do this!

Once I became comfortable breathing through the plastic tube, the water seemed to carry me along. All I had to do was kick my fins. This was way cool, but soon our time was up.

"Well, kids, good job out there." Maverick patted

me on the back after we returned to shore. "Especially you, Dominic. I'm proud of you. For your first time snorkeling, you did great."

"Thanks, Maverick." I shrugged. "I could still use some practice, though."

"Sorry we didn't find any shipwrecks—maybe next time." Maverick looked down at his watch as he helped me remove my fins.

"Nice watch." It looked like the fancy kind sold at the diving store.

"It's actually a diving computer with GPS."

"Hey, maybe you can help me find a fishing hot spot?" Still dripping wet, I opened my backpack; pulling out the crumpled napkin to show Maverick the co-ordinates. "Any idea where this might be?"

"Let's see." He entered the latitude and longitude into the computer. "Looks like it leads about a quarter mile directly south of here."

"What?" *That's not what I expected.* "Are you sure you don't mean east, toward the lake?"

"Nope. This is pretty accurate. You'll have a hard

time catching fish in the woods. Enjoy the rest of the day." Maverick quickly excused himself when the next group of "Snorkies" arrived.

"How was it, Dominic?" Windsong jumped up from her blanket, brushing the sand off her clothes. "Did you have a groovy time or what?"

I gave her a hug. "I had the best time, ever! Thank you for buying the snorkel gear for me."

"You can use it on land, too. Just fill the tube with Orange Crush and you're good to go," she snorted. "Well, looks like you need to get some dry clothes on."

I shoved my feet into my sandals and grabbed my towel, still confused about the coordinates. I leaned in close to Forest and Sailor.

"Let's get cleaned up and meet at the fort. I want to pay the doctor a visit," I said.

"Why? Are you feeling sick from swallowing all that lake water?" Sailor cocked an eyebrow.

Poor Sailor, God love'er.

After I exchanged my wet clothes for dry ones, I headed over the hill to our private beach where Forest and Sailor were impatiently waiting for me.

"Why do you want to talk to Dr. Goggles?" Forest asked. "More importantly, remind me why we have to meet in this dilapidated fort?"

"I just think there's more to his story," I sighed. "As for the fort, let's not lose sight of the trees for the forest, Forest."

"I never understood what that meant." He dodged a stick that fell from the roof.

"Anyone for a Tootsie Pop?" Sailor pulled three from her pocket.

"That's what *I'm* talking about." Forest sat back up, grabbing a cherry-flavored one from her hands.

"Thanks, Sailor." I unwrapped my orange sucker. "This might help spark some imagination."

"Like what? The Tootsie Roll should be on the outside?"

"Really, Forest?" I crumpled my wrapper, stuffing it in my pocket. "Now listen, guys. This Dr. Lloyd character seems to be holding back some information about the compass. Don't you find it strange that suddenly an intellectual professor shows up out of nowhere and starts hanging out with the Buckleys?"

"Sure do. So, what's the plan, Sherlock?" Forest already had his sucker chewed down to the stick.

"Head over and check this guy out. We're invited, after all."

We followed the trail that led through the park to the lighthouse. An enclosed staircase spiraled upward to the circular lamp room on top of the skeleton frame. Next door stood the three-story lightkeepers' dwelling where Dr. Lloyd was staying—a quaint white structure with a red roof and a round tower at one end.

We left the path, making our way across the lawn.

"Halt! Don't anybody move."

CHAPTER 8

We stopped dead in our tracks at the sight of Ranger Rick pointing a long-handled shovel right at us.

"Hey, take it easy with that," Forest said.

"Don't they teach you how to read in Illinois?"

I guess Ranger Rick still can't get past the fact that they're from out of state.

"The sign says, 'NO TRESPASSING,' and you crossed the line."

"We only wanted to tell Dr. Lloyd about what Dominic found in the lake."

Sailor! Forest and I glared at her simultaneously as she covered her mouth.

"Oh, really?" Ranger Rick cut through her with his icy stare. "And what might that be?"

"A … a pair of dentures," she said, hesitantly. "We thought his were missing."

Ranger Rick shook his head. "If I find you breaking the law again, I'm writing three citations. Am I making myself clear?"

"Clear as night, Officer," Forest said with a straight face.

"Good. Now I can't be babysitting you city slickers all day. I have work to do." He continued through the grounds carrying his shovel.

"There goes the gravedigger." Sailor tried to stifle her laughter. "Probably off digging three holes right now."

"All you need to worry about is not spilling the beans again." Forest tugged on one of Sailor's pigtails. She took a swing at him and missed.

"You two don't need to fight, the shipwreck was covered in so much green slime—I could've easily convinced him it was your camper down there."

We backtracked and came up to the lighthouse dwelling from the opposite direction. The door opened before we could knock.

"Hello, children. I had a feeling you'd show up. Come this way." Dr. Lloyd, clad in a long, white lab coat, waved his hand toward the hallway and stepped aside to let us in.

The interior looked quite ordinary until we reached the kitchen. Beakers and scientific gadgets covered the countertops; the table was lost under a stack of papers and files.

Dr. Lloyd slid his glasses on top of his bushy head. "As you can see, I've conducted some very extensive research while at Point Beach."

"That's why we're here, we're conducting some research of our own and wondered if you had time to finish telling us about the *Nellie Johnson*, and why you think Pirate Dan Seavey tried to steal it," I said.

"Very well, if you must know—the *Nellie Johnson* was carrying cedar posts. Seavey was a timber pirate of the Great Lakes."

"That must be where the expression 'Shiver me timbers' came from," Forest joked.

"You mean the booty was just a bunch of logs? What's so great about that?" Sailor's shoulders dropped.

"That's not all, my dear. What was beneath the posts was even more valuable," Dr. Lloyd explained. "You see, McCormick was hiding something."

"Like what?" My eyes widened.

"Klondike gold." Dr. Lloyd put a finger aside his mouth to silence our surprise. "Few knew that Dan Seavey and R.J. McCormick were partners during the gold rush. Dan became suspicious after their expedition went bust, but R. J. came back rich — especially if he could afford a 41-ton vessel like *Nellie*. Dan soon discovered that R.J. was using her to transport the rest of the gold to the bank."

"If that's the case, then it would only be fair for him to hijack the ship to even the score," I reasoned. "But I thought you said it caught fire?"

"I did … except I didn't say which ship." Dr. Lloyd began wandering through the room. "Has anyone seen my glasses?"

"They're on top of your head," I pointed out.

Forest rolled his eyes and made a "cuckoo" sign, circling a finger around his ear.

"Oh, yes. Now let's see here." He reached for a file, sifting through a pile of research papers and documents as we gathered around. "Aha. This is the report from the Coast Guard captain on the *Tuscarora* after the arrest."

> *June 26, 1908, I have the honor to confirm the capture of prisoner Pirate Dan Seavey on schooner Wanderer at high seas, approximately five miles N. E. Rawley Point. Nellie Johnson, found with six feet of water in her hold, was left in the possession of the lawful owner, R. J. McCormick, along with all her cargo.*

"From this, we can ascertain that Seavey switched ships and boarded *Wanderer* while R. J. was reunited with his own vessel. We can also determine that since *Nellie* was waterlogged, Seavey would've had to transport the treasure by another means."

"Like *Wanderer*." My detective skills sharpened.

"You're smart as a whip, my boy."

I smiled until Forest gave me a shove.

"Wait a minute, Einstein. That's *if* the treasure even made it that far. It could've ended up anywhere. Besides, who knows if the gold is even a fact."

"All my theories are based on facts, and soon I will prove how accurate they are." Dr. Lloyd stretched his hands in the air. "I'm on the brink of discovery!"

He reached for a large scrapbook, opening it to a page with a photo of a man in a captain's hat and suit. It was a mug shot labeled "Dan Seavey: Lake Pirate."

Sailor stared. "Roaring Dan doesn't look so bad. I'd say he looks *nice*, even. See, here—he's smiling."

"Yeah, well, looks can be deceiving," Forest argued. "He went to jail, didn't he?"

"Actually," Dr. Lloyd continued, "Dan got off the hook when R. J. failed to show up in court. He denied all acts of piracy, and was set free, landing ashore in Two Rivers only a few days later with some unfinished business."

"Roaring Dan must've gone back for the gold." I concocted my own theory. "And since R.J. wasn't in court, he was probably looking for it too."

"I've already considered that, although I have reason to believe that Seavey scuttled the ship — meaning he deliberately tried to sink it."

"Why would he do such a thing?" Sailor held up her palms.

"To keep the gold out of the wrong hands," Dr. Lloyd answered.

Dr. Lloyd turned the page to a photo of a schooner with sails hoisted high, and a cannon on deck. "Ah, *Wanderer*." His eyes came to life. "Nothing is on record of the pirate ship — she simply vanished."

"Someone must know what happened," I said. "If this was really big news at the time, then people would be watching."

"That's why I'm here." Dr. Lloyd took a seat in an overstuffed chair, crossing his legs. "To solve the mystery and finish my book. I'll become famous!"

"Maybe this person can help." I decided to put my faith in him and handed over the card from Diver Dan that I'd kept in my pocket for safekeeping.

He glanced at it. "Preposterous," he sneered. "I'm not interested in your childish imaginations." He crumpled the card, tossing it on the floor. "After all my time and effort—you would turn history into just another tourist trap?"

Ouch. I guess he shared the same sentiment as Captain Bill when it came to diving enthusiasts.

"Either way, I'm sure Dan didn't leave any gold lying around for the taking," Forest added.

"But if he did—I bet there's a map," I said, feeling like I knew a thing or two about pirates.

"That's why I'm so interested in the compass." Dr. Lloyd walked over to a table with a wide cylinder containing a clear liquid. Inside, fizzing bubbles formed around the compass, floating to the surface.

"What are you doing with that?" Sailor leaned in for a closer look.

"Simple," he explained. "I've immersed the compass in a ten percent nitric acid solution to remove deposits that formed on the exposed metal over time."

Dr. Lloyd put on safety goggles and a pair of

thin, latex gloves. Using a metal forceps, he lifted the chain, dipping the compass up and down several times before removing it from the liquid.

"Artifacts of this nature must be treated very delicately," he explained, while rubbing a cloth over the tarnished metal.

We watched closely as Dr. Lloyd carefully lifted the cover. I could barely read the numbered orientation lines that ran around the outer edge of the compass from behind the clouded glass. The magnetic needle was pointing in the north position, but nothing appeared to be pointing to Roaring Dan or the gold.

There were four pins, equally spaced around the outer rim of the compass. Dr. Lloyd pressed his thumb against the pin at the bottom, which caused the lens to slide open. He inspected a slot on the inside of the device. Inserting a small screwdriver, he turned it counterclockwise. Out popped a secret compartment.

There was something inside.

CHAPTER 9

Dr. Lloyd carefully removed a small piece of faded paper from within the hidden compartment of the compass. We watched as he pulled back each fold with a tweezers.

"Just as I suspected—a map!" He stared intently through bifocals which nearly collided with his protruding eyebrows.

"See, I knew it!" I stood victorious.

The map was divided by lines like a grid that covered both land and water features, with an arrow pointed to a capital "N" at the top. The rest was difficult to make out.

"By the looks of it, the gold could be anywhere, even on shore." Forest peered over his shoulder.

"Dominic has a metal detector!" Sailor became ecstatic. "We can help you look for the gold."

"You've helped me enough, already." Dr. Lloyd

pulled the map out of view. "I need to do a bit more research. Leave me now. You can come back tomorrow."

We left the lighthouse feeling encouraged, except for the part where Dr. Lloyd insinuated that I was a child.

"You should've shown him the badge." Sailor's eyes narrowed at Forest.

"No way. It probably would've ended up in the trash along with Diver Dan's business card." Forest pretended to crumple the card in his hands and toss it over his shoulder. "I think he was just giving us the run-around, trying to find out if we knew anything."

"Let's take this up tomorrow, guys." I was ready to call it a day. "Meet me back here at eight o'clock. Then we can see how the treasure hunt's going."

"Only this time, let's come in from the beach side," Sailor suggested. "I don't want Ranger Rick catching us again."

We fist-bumped each other before splitting up.

When I got back to camp, I found Grandpa Bob sitting at the fire pit with a birdwatcher magazine, black smoke curling from the heated logs.

"Hey, GB, I need to get an early start tomorrow. Can you wake me up before eight?"

"Are you feeling okay? It's not like you to get up before the crack of noon."

"Yes, I'm fine. Dr. Lloyd needs our help with his research." I decided to keep things vague. I didn't want him spoiling the expedition.

"Too bad you'll miss out on the Canasta tournament. I know how much you love card games."

Oh, no. Such a shame …

GB doused the fire. "Well, Dominic, when life gives you options, and sleep is one of them—I always choose sleep."

"Thanks, GB. I'll remember that."

After downing three of Mom's molasses cookies and a glass of milk—GB's idea of making sure I didn't get homesick—I climbed into my cot and closed my eyes, thinking about how great it would be to discover pirate's booty at Point Beach. I tried to get some shut-eye, but my mind was too restless.

Instead, I turned on my flashlight, which only partially lit. After shaking it up and down a few times, it brightened a little.

I swear these things are more like containers for holding dead batteries.

Reaching for my backpack, I grabbed *Treasures of the Great Lakes*, thinking it might help me fall asleep. As I shuffled through the pages, I noticed many photographs of people in diving suits and underwater images of sunken ships. There was even a chapter about pirates and crooks, with the same mug shot of Roaring Dan, front and center. I dog-eared the page.

Beneath it was a picture of a young boy on a dock wearing a star-shaped badge pinned to his vest. It looked exactly like the one Forest found on the beach.

The name under the caption was Charlie Vinnette ... *Sadie's father!*

Charlie even gave a statement to the press:

"When I asked Roaring Dan what he did with the treasure, his response was, 'What any good pirate would do—I buried it.' Then he gave me this badge and told me to keep it a secret."

Hmmm ... Mrs. Buckley probably knows a lot more than she's letting on. I wondered if Dr. Lloyd knew about this.

I could hear the pitter-patter of rain pelting off Nimrod's thin walls; a crack of thunder echoing through the trees. For the longest time I remained wide awake—partially thanks to GB's diabolical snoring, but his rattling wheezes were no match for the rushing winds blowing off Lake Michigan.

A storm was brewing at Point Beach.

CHAPTER 10

The next morning, I woke up in a cold sweat on the floor. "What just happened?"

"You had a bad dream." Grandpa Bob stood over me. "I heard you tossing back and forth. You were mumbling about a gravedigger, and the next thing I know, you're screaming— 'He's got the gold!' That's when I got up and found you on the floor."

"Oh, brother." I held my head. "I must've fallen out of bed. What time is it?"

"Half past seven. Let's have some grub, and then we have work to do. That storm last night dropped some mighty big branches into the campsite. When nature hands you free firewood, you don't complain."

Moaning, I rubbed my eyes. Two questions immediately came to mind: One—did this "grub" involve SPAM? And two—where was the log cabin GB built last night when he sawed all those logs?

"Okay, okay, Grandpa. Geez. Between your snoring and the storm, I barely slept." Yawning, I reached for my bunny slippers—Mom's warped attempt to coddle her teenage boy. They were super comfy. If only they weren't pink.

"Butter the toast, kiddo. The scrambled eggs are almost ready." GB tossed two plates onto the table and turned to flip the eggs, scooping a pile onto my plate.

I was just about to take a bite of toast when I noticed GB's eyes were closed and his hands were folded. Either he was dozing off, or about to pray. I went with the latter and followed suit.

"Dear Lord, we thank you for this food on our table and for keeping us safe during the storm. We also appreciate Your provision of the firewood. Amen."

I nodded in agreement, scarfing down my eggs. I didn't want to be late, and I still had a whole yard of sticks and branches to pick up.

Once we'd loaded GB's truck with enough kindling wood to last a whole summer of campfires, I raced down the road toward the lighthouse on my bike

to save time. Forest and Sailor were already there looking for me on the beach.

"Geez, Dominic. You made a big production about us showing up, and then it turns out we're wait-ing on you instead," Forest complained.

"Sorry, guys. I had a restless night. I think I had a case of insomnia." I hid my bike behind some bushes.

"Don't worry, Dominic. Insomnia is nothing to lose sleep over," Sailor said. "Lots of people get it."

Forest shook his head. "I'll pretend I didn't just hear you say that." He picked up a few flat rocks and whipped one across the waves. It skipped four times before it disappeared.

In the distance, I noticed a boat tunnel pass at low speed. It was the *Willie Bee*. I thought he usually stayed clear of this area, but I couldn't worry about that now.

"Just wait until you take a look at this!" I reached into my backpack for the treasure book, opening to the marked page. "Recognize anything?"

"Hey, it's my badge." Forest dropped his rocks.

"Yep. It used to belong to Dan Seavey, before he gave it to Sadie's dad. It says so right here …"

"What?" Forest leaned in closer.

"That's probably why Dr. Lloyd's trying to dig up information from Mrs. Buckley," I guessed. "I think we need to ask her a few questions ourselves, and I bet if you show her the badge, it'll jog her memory."

"I doubt it." Forest rolled his eyes. "But shouldn't we check in with the doctor first?"

"Good idea." I closed the book and was about to put it in my backpack, when I noticed an endorsement on the back cover from a peculiar-looking man with a crooked grin, named Dr. McCormick.

He looked all too familiar. On a hunch, I grabbed a black pen, adding dark-rimmed glasses, bushy hair, and a mustache to his features. *Could it be Dr. Lloyd?*

I shoved the book into my backpack, dropping it alongside my bike before joining Forest and Sailor who were making their way toward the lighthouse dwelling.

Oddly, the front door was unlocked, so we

peeked inside. "Dr. Lloyd?" I called through the crack.

No one answered as we entered the apartment on the ground floor and head straight to the mad scientist's laboratory. The once-orderly room was now in disarray.

"He must've left in a hurry to forget these." Forest lifted a pair of black-rimmed safety goggles.

"Something doesn't feel right about this." Sailor bit her nails.

"Hey, guys, look what I found." I picked up a large book, dusting off the cover. "It's the lightkeeper's logbook from 1908, the same year as the arrest."

I turned to the entry page after the alert from the U.S. Coast Guard was received and started reading aloud:

June 25th A severe storm with a northeast wind blowing at forty to fifty mph. caused a wild goose to strike the tower clock room.

"Poor thing," Sailor whimpered.

"Not only that. I bet the storm's what caused *Nel-*

lie to get waterlogged, and that's why Dan Seavey abandoned ship at the Two Rivers port," I deduced.

"So, it wasn't 'fowl' play?" Forest joked.

"You could say that. Let's keep reading and see what else we find." I turned the page and continued:

> *June 26th 9:23 a.m. Schooner Wanderer was forced onto a sand bar, spotted due east off Rawley Point where Pirate Dan Seavey was captured and taken aboard the Tuscarora.*

> *10:05 a.m. Wanderer capsized, after which Captain R. J. McCormick was rescued by local fishermen in a Mackinaw boat. He remains in the lighthouse dwelling, crazed with sickness and in search of a compass he reported lost at sea.*

"Looks like my theory was right." I closed the book. "While Dan's being hauled off to jail, McCormick boarded *Wanderer* with the compass—probably trying to recapture the gold, I'm guessing."

"What does all this mean?" Sailor twisted her long, blonde braids in a knot.

"It means your ship left port a long time ago," Forest scoffed. He punched her in the arm.

Just then, there came a light rap on the door.

"Yoo-hoo, Dr. Lloyd!" Mrs. Buckley's voice rang through the corridor. The aroma of freshly baked snickerdoodles filled the air.

"Hi, Mrs. Buckley." Sailor scooped up Sprinkles who was in a deliriously happy poodle state, greeting her with doggie kisses. "Dr. Lloyd's not here. Do you think he got kidnapped?"

"Oh my, you children have a great deal of imagination," Sadie chuckled. "He's probably gone on another adventure. Would anyone like a cookie?"

"No, thanks." *Who could eat at a time like this?*

"Alright, who are you and what did you do with Dominic?" Forest nudged me in the ribs, handing me the badge. "Now's your chance."

"Umm, Mrs. Buckley … can you look at this?"

She studied the dull piece of metal in her trembling hands. "Heavens, where did you find it?"

"Forest found it on the beach right next to site #127. We kept it a secret because we thought we had broken the law. The ranger said I needed a permit for my metal detector, and I didn't have one."

Sadie sighed as she handed it back to me. "My father once had a badge like this, but it's too old and worn to know if this is the same one or not."

"I have an idea." I put on Dr. Lloyd's safety goggles, dropping the badge into the container of solution. Bubbles fizzed over the corroded metal, revealing two letters. "There's something etched on the back—C. V."

"Seavey?" Forest assumed.

"No dear, those are my father's initials—Charlie Vinnette. When he was young, he wanted to be a pirate just like Dan. Later on, he'd take out the badge and let me wear it when we played pretend cops and robbers on the beach."

"Did he ever mention anything about Roaring Dan's treasure?" I asked.

"The truth is, Dan gave all his money to the poor

before he died—on Valentine's Day, no less—but left behind his most valued possession for my dad."

"Was it gold?" Sailor gasped.

"No, sugar plum—it was his Bible." Sadie lifted the lid on her picnic basket, producing a thick, soft-covered book with worn pages.

"I guess Roaring Dan had a change of heart after all." Forest sounded convinced. "But why didn't you tell Dr. Lloyd sooner?"

She leaned forward in childlike innocence. "I was so caught up in his stories that I wanted to believe there really *was* buried treasure, just as you did, but if Dr. Lloyd continues this silly quest, I'm afraid he'll be greatly disappointed."

Sadie plumped down into a chair; a small piece of paper fluttered to the floor. I picked it up.

"A map! It came out of the Bible."

Forest and Sailor crowded in. A stretch of dashed lines traversed across the water that led from a spot on shore marked with a star, to an image of a ship with three sails.

"Funny, I never noticed that before." Sadie looked bewildered. "My dad like to bury treasure for me to find using maps exactly like this one."

My eyes widened. "Can I have it?"

"Sure, but don't get too excited," she said, waving her finger. "It was mostly just trinkets, and sometimes allowance money. My father often said Seavey's treasure was right here in this canon."

She pulled the bookmark out from the Bible, pointing out the highlighted verse. "*Your heart will always be where your treasures are. Matthew 6:21.*"

"Wait a minute—say that again?" I asked.

"Your heart will always …"

"No, I mean the part about what your father told you," I clarified.

"Seavey's treasure is in the canon?"

"That's it!" I blurted. "Mrs. Buckley, can you do us a favor?" I prayed she was up to the task. "Can you find Maverick and ask him to meet us on the beach?"

"I suppose I can do that."

"Thanks for the help, Mrs. B., but we gotta run."

CHAPTER 11

"Dominic, do you mind cluing us in?" Forest asked.

I pulled my bike and backpack out of the bushes. "Don't you get it? The treasure's in the cannon—the cannon of a ship! One of us needs to get the snorkel gear."

"Way ahead of you, Dom—I'll meet you on the beach." Forest sped off on my bike while Sailor and I made our way to the lake.

"But how will we find the ship?" Sailor asked.

"By using Charlie's map, and if the wreck is the same one I saw from the *Willie Bee*, then it's not far from shore. We should be able to get to it."

Once we arrived at the beach, I pulled out the map and orientated it to line up with the north directional arrow, using the lighthouse to find our bearing.

"We must be pretty close," I determined.

Treasure Map
W
S
N
E

The shoreline was void of the usual picnickers and swimmers. Tumbling waves brought in bits of debris from last night's storm, making the water look even more uninviting.

Just as I established our position, Forest showed up with a large duffle bag. We put on our life jackets and snorkel gear and waded into the lake.

"I wish Maverick was here." Sailor shivered. "I have a bad feeling about this."

"We'll be fine. Besides, I'm sure Mrs. Buckley found him by now. He should be on his way."

But was I sure? In my mind, I could picture her driving around the campground in circles, with Sprinkles barking at anything that moved.

"Let's spread out to cover more territory. It should be straight ahead." I placed the breathing tube in my mouth. After the initial shock of the freezing water wore off, I took two big steps and dove in.

The waves were rough, making me feel a little less confident. I noticed the lake bottom seemed to drop off and then come back up again. That must be what Captain Bill meant by a "shoal." I soon realized I couldn't touch bottom anymore, though the shore was far enough away that I didn't think about going back. The shipwreck had to be out here, somewhere.

After a while, I came up for a breather to check on the others. Forest swam over, treading water alongside me, but Sailor had veered off course.

Suddenly, she lifted her head out of the water and began bobbing up and down. Out came an unrecognizable sound — "Wye wow wit!"

"Take your mouthpiece out, Sailor," Forest yelled to her as we swam over to see what the fuss was about.

"I found it!" she sputtered. "The sunken ship!"

The three of us gathered around a dark image on the bottom of the lake. The wreck was covered in mussels and algae; some of the wood planks had pulled loose and scattered over the sand. Most of the rigging was still in place, but the main mast lay broken on the deck where a school of small fish flitted past.

Could it be Wanderer? I was hoping to find the

cannon onboard but searching below deck wasn't something we could do as amateurs.

"I can hardly believe it—we found the ship!" Forest shouted as we resurfaced. "We need to go back and tell someone."

"Wait a minute, what's that over there?" Sailor pointed. The sun poked through the clouds, glinting off a shiny object floating nearby.

"It must be a fishing buoy," I assumed, thinking back to when I saw the *Willie Bee* earlier. "I have an idea. We could use it to mark the wreck. I'll go get it."

Did I just say that?

I went back underwater, trying to keep an eye on the buoy as it bobbed up and down in the waves, beckoning for me to come and find it.

When I finally reached the buoy, I pulled up on the rope, but it wouldn't budge. I put my head down below water to get a closer look. *What's this?* It was hooked on a net that was tangled around ... a cannon!

I thought back to what Mrs. Buckley said at the lighthouse dwelling. *The treasure is in the cannon.*

It was only a few feet from the surface, so without giving it another thought, I removed my life vest, pushing my way to the bottom to get closer.

When I reached for the barrel of the cannon, something pulled on my fin. It kept tugging me downward, until water started to fill my breathing tube. I tried to kick my way up, but I couldn't.

I was caught in the net!

Don't panic, Dominic. I held my breath. Thinking quickly, I unfastened the fin and was able to squeeze my foot out and resurface, but the current continued to grab me and pull me under.

I kept trying to break free of its grasp, but with only one fin, I felt more like a lame duck. Frantically, I looked toward shore while fighting against the force of the waves, only to find the beach was empty. *Rescue me, Lord …*

Then, out of nowhere, a boat appeared.

It was the *Thirsty Tiger*.

CHAPTER 12

"Give me your hand!" The bronze-skinned lady, sporting a black wetsuit reached over the side of the boat.

I had no choice but to grab onto her as I struggled to the ladder. I slid over the sidewall, collapsing onto the deck.

"Looks like you were in a bit of a pickle, my boy." A man in khaki shorts with white loafers leaned over me. I recognized him.

"Dr. Lloyd?" I gasped. "What are you doing here? Are you alright?"

"The question is, are *you* alright?"

"I'm fine, but what are you doing with Thirsty Tiger lady?" I could finally breathe again and had enough strength to sit up.

"Oh, you mean Katrina." He started pacing. "I decided to call Diving Adventures after all, since I was in need of a boat with specialized equipment. The owner set me up with Miss Carter at the marina, but I'm beginning to think it was a mistake."

"What are you children doing out here, unattended?" Katrina frowned as Forest and Sailor climbed into the boat behind me. "Don't you know how much danger you were in?"

"We were just going for a swim." Sailor stood in a puddle of water on the deck. "What are you doing with Dr. Lloyd?"

"I've been commissioned by the Federal Marine Archaeology Department to investigate suspicious activity involving the exploitation of artifacts. He's being held for questioning." She stared intently at us. "You three aren't involved, I hope?"

Dr. Lloyd's face turned bright red. "What? That's outrageous."

"Settle down and take a seat, everyone. You too, Mr. Soggy," Katrina sternly advised.

"It's SAH-gee, and what do you mean, exploiting artifacts?" he demanded.

This was *not* a good situation. I glanced over my

shoulder toward Point Beach. A few people began to appear at the water's edge, but no Maverick or Sadie.

"Wait a minute." Katrina looked us over, turning her attention onto me. "I recognize you. You're the kid I ran into at the diving store … the one who snagged my shipwreck marker."

"Are you sure?" My heart raced. "I'm pretty average—lots of kids my age look like me."

"Can someone please explain what's going on?" Forest rubbed his neck. "Dominic almost drowned out there, and now we're being treated like criminals or something."

"Don't worry, children. Simple folk don't understand scholarly work such as this." Dr. Lloyd glared at Miss Carter. "I'm an esteemed member of society, and I demand you take us back immediately."

"That doesn't change the fact that taking artifacts off of shipwrecks is illegal." She dropped the anchor.

"I explained to you a thousand times. The compass was surrendered to me. I didn't steal it." He pointed a finger at her. "This woman is after my gold."

"*Your* gold?" She laughed. "Save it for the judge."

"Do you have any idea who I am?" Dr. Lloyd leaned forward, eyes slanted. Then I noticed his hairline begin to shift and slide too far to one side.

"*I* do, Dr. Sogge, or should I say … *McCormick.*" I ran up to him, pulling off his hairpiece and mustache before he realized what was happening, but when I tried to pull off his unibrow, he yelped.

"Oops, sorry about that." I didn't realize his eyebrows were real.

"How did I miss this?" Katrina stood back. "Dr. McCormick, I'm one of your biggest fans. Your research has helped me a great deal."

"But what's with the disguise?" I asked.

"Let me explain …" His eyes sank. "I changed my identity, because my great-uncle, R.J., was known for telling wild stories, and I couldn't afford to lose my credentials. After years of trying to recover the gold, he lost his marbles. I knew if I could find the treasure, it would set things right, until Miss Carter stepped in."

"Well, I'm trying to preserve the maritime history

of the Great Lakes, just as you are," Katrina added.

We were so distracted that I never noticed a kayak had glided up to the *Thirsty Tiger*.

"Hey, Kat. Looks like you're having a party but forgot to invite me." Maverick paddled alongside us.

"Did one of your snorkel lessons get out of hand, Maverick?" Katrina put a hand on her hip. "These kids were caught in a rip current, and I had to rescue them."

"I think I know what they were up to." Maverick raised my fin. "Is one of you missing something?"

I froze, speechless.

"It was caught in a gill net that just so happened to be floating by a shipwreck," Maverick added. "But I don't suppose any of you noticed that?"

Forest and Sailor shrunk in their seats.

"You knew the wreck was there all along." I confronted him. "Why did you lie about the GPS location?"

"Besides my job at Point Beach this summer, I'm also working with Katrina as an intern." Maverick tied his kayak to the anchor rope. "I knew she wouldn't appreciate three children tampering with evidence, so I had to do my utmost to keep it a secret."

"I suspect we're all in the same boat—no pun intended." Dr. Lloyd shrugged. "Each one of us wants to find the gold."

"Maybe our three detectives would like to share what they know?" Maverick turned to us.

Sailor fanned herself with her hands. "Oh, Maverick, there's nothing in this world I wouldn't do for you."

Does anyone have some Pepto Bismal? I think I'm going to be sick.

"We used C. V.'s map to find the ship," Forest said.

"Impossible. I have the only map." Dr. Lloyd folded his arms.

"This one came from C.V.—Charlie Vinnette," I explained. "We left it on the beach."

"That figures." Dr. Lloyd tapped his foot. "I knew the Buckleys were holding back information."

"Dominic thinks that Roaring Dan hid the gold in the cannon," Forest interjected.

"Unfortunately, Diver Dan already explored the mystery wreck," Katrina said. "It didn't hold a cannon on board, or anything else that would lead us to believe it carried a cache of gold, nor could he confirm it was *Wanderer*."

"That's because only Charlie knew Roaring Dan's secret. The reports had things confused. He pushed the cannon overboard, not Captain McCormick." I pointed to the buoy. "It's right over there."

"Dominic, you found the cannon!" Sailor ran up and hugged me.

"Good work, lad." Dr. Lloyd nodded in approval.

"How could we miss this?" Katrina looked at Maverick. "We scoured the entire area."

"The sand must've shifted during last night's storm," Dr. Lloyd reasoned. "But what about the gold?"

"I guess there's only one way to find out." Maverick paddled over to the buoy.

Using the winch off the *Thirsty Tiger,* Katrina began to hoist up the cannon with a long chain. It strained under the weight, but once the artifact reached the surface, it was easily brought close enough to the boat.

Katrina moved toward it, but Dr. Lloyd, in his excitement, shoved her aside and pried open the plug at the end of the barrel, reaching inside.

He removed his hand and opened his fist to reveal a mound of gold nuggets, sparkling in his palm. "The treasure!" he shouted with glee.

"We're going to be rich!" Sailor leaped for joy, and I have to admit, I was caught up in the moment, too.

Even Forest couldn't contain himself, throwing a fist into the air — "Yesss!" he shouted.

Once our job was done, it was time to return to civilian life. Forest, Sailor, and I jumped back in the water and swam to shore, escorted by Maverick in his kayak. Bert and Sadie Buckley were waiting for us.

"Oh, I'm so relieved to see you're alright. I was beginning to think something terrible happened to all of you!" Sadie rubbed her temple.

"We found Roaring Dan's gold and the sunken ship, Mrs. Buckley, thanks to C. V.'s map." Sailor made her way over to them.

"Well, I'll be." Sadie's eyes grew big as saucers.

"These kids are something else." Maverick beached his kayak and joined the group. "We may never have found the treasure, if it wasn't for them."

"Maverick's helping with the research," Sailor said. "He's brave *and* smart."

Maverick grinned. "Now that I know everyone's safe and sound, I'd better get back to work."

Sailor's body went limp. She pressed her hand to her forehead. "Will I … I mean, will *we* ever see you again?"

Maverick gave her one of his famous Kool-Aid smiles before shoving his kayak back into the water.

I removed my snorkel gear, feeling a big sense of accomplishment.

"We're so proud of you," Sadie gushed. "And to think, the clue was right there in the Bible the whole time. My father would've been thrilled to know you found it."

"He led us to the shipwreck, but I can't help but

wonder if the 'star' on the map leads to something more." Forest grabbed the map from my backpack and studied it.

"I wouldn't be surprised," Mrs. Buckley agreed. "But I'm not sure where to begin; the landscape has changed so much over time."

"I think I can help with that." I pulled out the deputy badge.

CHAPTER 13

I felt confident leading the Buckleys to the dune behind site #127. "I'm guessing the 'star' on the map is where Forest found the badge."

"You mean we were close to finding Sadie's treasure?" Forest asked.

"That's what I think."

As we turned the corner, I heard the familiar sound of blips and beeps. I ran ahead; in the clearing I found Ranger Rick combing the ridge with *my* metal detector.

"Hey, what are you doing with that?" I demanded.

The ruckus must have interrupted the Canasta game—GB and Windsong came over the ridge from the other side. We had Ranger Rick surrounded.

"What in tarnation is going on over here?" GB stormed up to Ranger Rick, grabbing the metal detector from him. "Stealing from a kid, eh?"

"Now, see here, Nimrod. You don't interrogate the

law, got that?" Ranger Rick defiantly picked up his shovel, sticking it in the sand. "It's illegal to use a detector on state property unless you're an official."

"Gentlemen, please. Can we discuss this in a civilized manner?" Windsong wedged herself between them.

"I'm the one who found the treasure map." Ranger Rick pointed a finger to his chest. "I'm in charge here, so I'll be the one finding the gold, if you don't mind."

"I think you're a little late." Sadie hobbled over. "The gold's already been found. It came off a sunken ship. Now let these kids have their fun."

"Hogwash." Ranger Rick shook his head. "The map that Dr. Lloyd gave me clearly points to the shore but suit yourself—you won't find anything. I've been out here for days." He wiped the sweat from his forehead.

Finally, I had a chance to do what I came here for— hunt for buried treasure with my metal detector—or at least, anything other than bottle caps.

I surveyed the area until I spied the log. "This is

close to where Forest found the badge—I remember!"

I swung the detector left and right. Suddenly, it made a loud buzz. I tried to hone in on the sound.

"I knew it had to be around here, somewhere." Sadie clasped her hands together.

Forest started to dig with Ranger Rick's shovel. Bending down to loosen the dirt with his hands, he pulled up a small wooden chest, handing it to Sadie.

She carefully lifted the lid on the box. There was a jar inside with an array of trinkets and mementos. She opened it, removing a note.

"What does it say?" Ranger Rick crowded in.

"My dearest Sadie …" she read aloud, wiping a tear from her eye with her apron as she reached the end.

"Here, Mrs. Buckley." Forest handed her the badge. "I think this belongs to you."

"Why don't you keep it?" She handed it back.

"Are you sure?" he asked.

She smiled. "I will always have my memories."

My Dearest Sadie,

Congratulations on finding the pirate's booty! Keep up the good work, Sweetheart, and remember – the real treasure is always in your heart.

Love,
Dad

"Cheers to all the heroes who helped find the gold!" I raised my glass of Orange Crush in a toast. Forest, Sailor, Windsong, GB, the Buckleys, Maverick, Katrina, and Dr. Lloyd lifted their glasses to the center of the table, clinking them against mine.

"Congratulations to our three young detectives for making headline news in the Herald Times once more!" Windsong added, taking a sip of her iced tea.

We were celebrating our success at Port Sandy Bay restaurant with Wisconsin's best pizza.

"I hope you kids don't feel bad that you can't keep the gold. Remember, I did tell you earlier that this isn't a 'finders keepers' situation," Maverick said.

"It's 'finders keepers, *losers* weepers,'" Forest pointed out. "Why do we come out as losers? Shouldn't we get to keep at least some of it?" He slumped back in his chair.

"Sorry." Katrina shook her head. "The Abandoned Shipwreck Act of 1987 states that the U.S. Government has the right to claim any abandoned shipwreck submerged in U.S. waters and its possessions."

"I know it's disappointing, but just think what a great story you'll have to tell back home. You're heroes!" Maverick beamed.

"You'll always be *my* hero." Sailor had propped her elbow on the table, her hand cupping her face, eyes glued to Maverick while her pizza sat untouched on her plate.

"So, can someone please tell me what Ranger Rick was doing, digging all those holes on the beach? He wasn't actually looking for gold, was he?" GB reached for another slice of pepperoni pizza.

"I'm afraid so." Dr. Lloyd pointed out the empty pitcher to the waitress as she walked by. "The ranger seemed to have a touch of 'gold fever.' He would bring me coffee every morning as an excuse to get inside my lab, so I purposely planted a fake map as a diversion to keep him out of my hair."

"I'm just glad Dominic got his metal detector back." Windsong turned to Dr. Lloyd. "So, what will become of you, Doctor? Are you hoping to make any more discoveries in the Great Lakes?"

"Presently, I will accompany Ms. Carter back to Madison. The cannon and gold need to be meticulously documented and preserved before they can go on display at Manitowoc's, Maritime Museum." He waved his hands in a grandiose fashion.

"Dr. Lloyd, you've got cheese on your chin." I pointed to the gooey string of mozzarella on his face.

After we had our fill of pizza, we stood to say our goodbyes. Sadie got teary-eyed and Windsong pulled everyone in for a hug.

"We'll see you next summer!" I promised. "Who knows? Maybe there'll be another mystery to solve."

"If there is, I know a team of young detectives who'll be on the case." Maverick winked. "Wish I could be there, but I have my internship at the archeology department to return to. I'm afraid Katrina would miss me too much if I stayed here."

She smiled, giving him a friendly shove. "Not!"

Forest walked over to the Buckleys. "I wanted to thank you again, Mrs. B., for letting me keep the badge. I'll make sure to take good care of it."

He started walking away, then turned back. "One more thing—watch out for those big birds!"

"What's that about Big Bird?" Bert asked as he and Sadie started making their way to their car.

Leaving the parking lot, GB and I turned one last time to wave goodbye to Windsong, Forest, and Sailor. We were heading north, and they were heading south.

"Man, I'm going to miss them." I waved until Windsong's slime-mobile rolled out of sight. "But we'll see them again, right GB?"

"Yes, of course, Dominic. Good old Nimrod has plenty of life in her for a few more years of camping." GB cranked up the polkas and floored it.

I stared at the towering pines that lined the road on the way out. Everything in life changes; even people change, but there was one thing I knew I could count on—these old friends would be here to greet us again.

Debby lives in Maribel, Wisconsin. She's a member of Pens of Praise Christian writers' group and enjoys family gatherings, country life and the four seasons.

Kate lives in Branch, Wisconsin. She's a member of Pens of Praise Christian writers' group and a church accompanist. She enjoys spending time with her family.

Connect with us online at:

Facebook.com/MysteryatPointBeach

Facebook.com/TheTinCanSeries

Thanks to all who helped put this book together, especially Sarah Grosskopf, Anne Bender, and Mike Oswald. We would also like to thank Ben Wolf, our editor, Tony Mukiibi Ebenezer for designing the map, and Isaac Mugerwa for designing our website.

Books in the Mystery at Point Beach Series:

Book 1: Sundae Wars

Book 2: Pirate's Booty

Book 3: Alien Invasion

Book 4: Bushwhacked

Book 5: The Ringmaster

Book 6: Haunted Hemlock

Books in The Tin Can Series:

Book 1: Mystery at Flamingo Bay